He could draw his way out of *any* danger! He *always* saved the day.

PAWS McDRAW

~ THE FASTEST DOODLER IN THE WEST ~

CONNAH BRECON

LITTLE TIGER PRESS
London

Meet Paws McDraw.
The fastest doodler in the west!

So when the bunnies were in trouble who did they turn to? Paws McDraw!

At the well, Timmy was in trouble. Deep trouble.

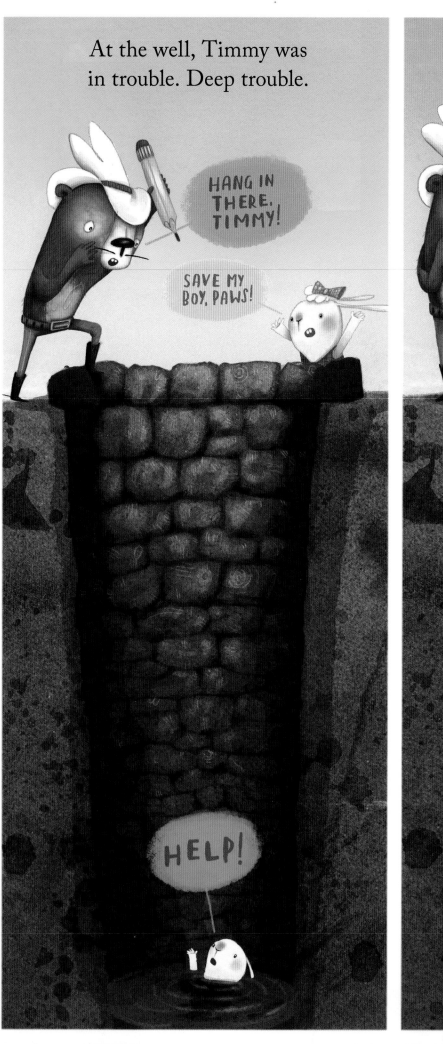

Paws pulled out his pencil and started to sketch.

Then he pulled Timmy
up, up, up to safety!

WOO HOO

"Hooray for Paws McDraw!"
cried the bunnies when Timmy
was high and dry.

They carried their hero
home to celebrate.

WELCOME
BUNNY HILL
HOME OF THE
CUPCAKE
POP: 656,000,000 A LOT!

The bunnies threw a crazy cupcake carnival
in Paws' honour.

(Because y'all know bunnies
LOVE cupcakes, right?)

What an extravaganza of icing and sprinkles it was! Everyone was having a rootin'-tootin' time until . . .

. . . in burst
the Rascally Raccoon Gang.

Those lean, mean cupcake rustlers
started terrorising the town!

Paws knew what had to be done.

Someone had to stop the raccoons.

And that someone was *him*.

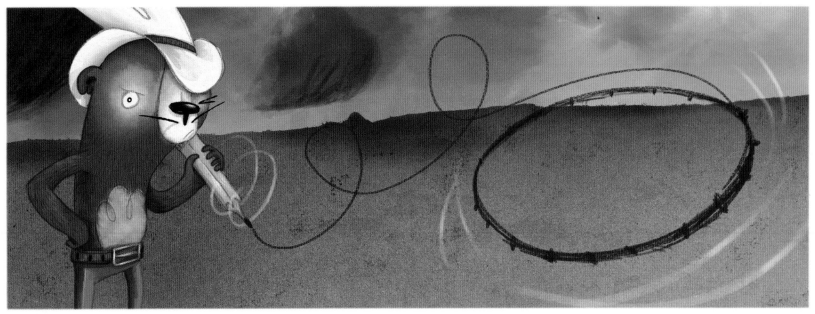

Paws was quick on the draw. He started to doodle . . .

and soon those raccoons were all tied up!

But in the blink of an eye,
they'd snipped their way free!
Paws needed a new plan. And fast.

He sharpened his lead and sketched as quickly as he could.

And before you could say hot-diggity-dawg,
Paws had those rascally raccoons . . .

. . . all locked up!

They were licked.

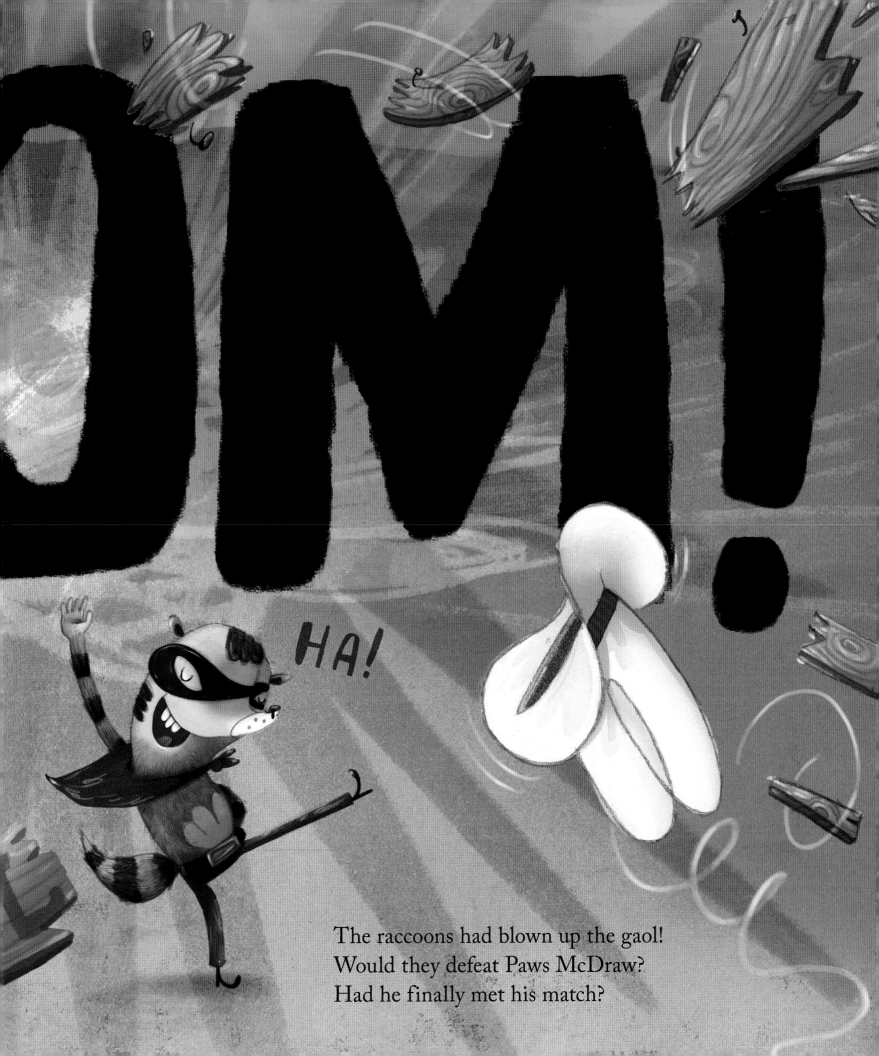

The raccoons had blown up the gaol!
Would they defeat Paws McDraw?
Had he finally met his match?

Paws was in real trouble! He was out of ideas! He needed a recipe for success!!

And, as the baker handed him his pencil, Paws had a brainwave.

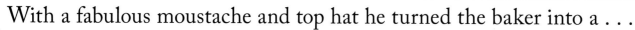

With a fabulous moustache and top hat he turned the baker into a . . .

HEY PESTO!
mix lightly
FOCUS POCUS!
GAS mark 3
FABRACADABRA!
BUTTER-CREAM
AND
SPRINKLES
ON TOP!

With a swish of his wand and a few magic words the baker turned those terrible raccoons into . . .

"Woo hoo!" cried the bunnies as they chased the not-so-Rascally Raccoon cupcakes out of town.

Yup, Paws had saved the day again!
(With a bit of help from his friends.)

Three cheers for mighty
Paws McDraw!